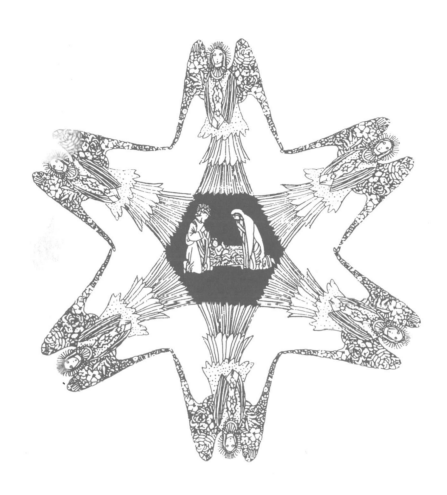

For little Ornella

OXFORD
UNIVERSITY PRESS

Great Clarendon Street, Oxford OX2 6DP

Oxford University Press is a department of the University of Oxford.
It furthers the University's objective of excellence in research, scholarship,
and education by publishing worldwide in

Oxford   New York

Auckland   Cape Town   Dar es Salaam   Hong Kong   Karachi
Kuala Lumpur   Madrid   Melbourne   Mexico City   Nairobi
New Delhi   Shanghai   Taipei   Toronto

With offices in
Argentina   Austria   Brazil   Chile   Czech Republic   France   Greece
Guatemala   Hungary   Italy   Japan   Poland   Portugal   Singapore
South Korea   Switzerland   Thailand   Turkey   Ukraine   Vietnam

Oxford is a registered trade mark of Oxford University Press
in the UK and in certain other countries

British Library Cataloguing in Publication Data
Data available

ISBN: 978-0-19-272730-5

3 5 7 9 10 8 6 4

Printed in China

Paper used in the production of this book is a natural,
recyclable product made from wood grown in sustainable forests.
The manufacturing process conforms to the environmental
regulations of the country of origin.

Brian Wildsmith

A Christmas Story

OXFORD
UNIVERSITY PRESS

Once, a long time ago, in a town called Nazareth, a little donkey was born.

When the little donkey was almost nine months old, his mother set out on a long journey with her mistress and master, whose names were Mary and Joseph.

They asked Rebecca, who lived next door to them,
to look after the little donkey while they were gone.

But the little donkey was very sad without his
mother and refused to eat. So Rebecca packed food and water
and promised the little donkey that they would find his mother.

And they set out
to follow Mary and Joseph.

The roads were full of people travelling to various towns and cities.
'Have you seen a donkey with a man and a woman?' Rebecca asked a traveller.
'Yes, they passed me on the road to Jerusalem,' the traveller replied.

Rebecca and the little
donkey took the road to
Jerusalem. Soon they came
to a soldier standing guard
at a splendid palace.
'Have you seen a donkey with
a man and a woman?' Rebecca
asked the soldier.
'Yes, they passed this way,'
the soldier answered.
'Now hurry along. There are
important visitors here to see
King Herod.'

Rebecca and the little donkey continued on their way.
In time, they met some shepherds keeping watch over their flocks.
'Have you seen a donkey with a man and a woman?' Rebecca asked them.

'Yes, they were going towards Bethlehem,'
the shepherds replied.

So the little donkey and Rebecca went on.
Suddenly glorious music filled the sky. And then
they saw a great star shining down on the little town
of Bethlehem.

When they reached Bethlehem, they met a man
standing in the doorway of an inn. Rebecca asked if he
had seen Mary and Joseph and the donkey.

'Yes,' he replied. 'They wanted to
stay here, but there was no room
at the inn. They went to the stable.'
And the innkeeper showed
Rebecca the way.

The stable was bathed in a wonderful light
that shone from the bright star above.
As Rebecca and the little donkey came near,
they heard the sounds of a mother donkey
braying and a little baby crying.

Rebecca and the little donkey entered the stable and saw Mary and Joseph and the mother donkey. And there, lying in a manger, was a new-born baby.

'What are you going to call him?' asked Rebecca.
'His name is Jesus,' Mary replied.

In the days that followed, the little donkey and his mother went with Mary and Joseph and the baby Jesus into Egypt. And Rebecca rode home on a king's camel.

And it came to pass that Mary and Joseph returned to Nazareth,
and there Jesus grew up, with Rebecca as his friend.

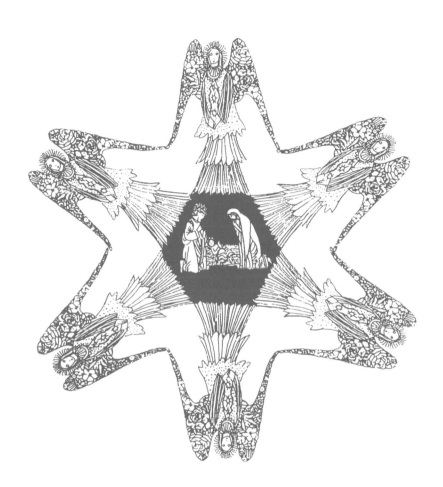

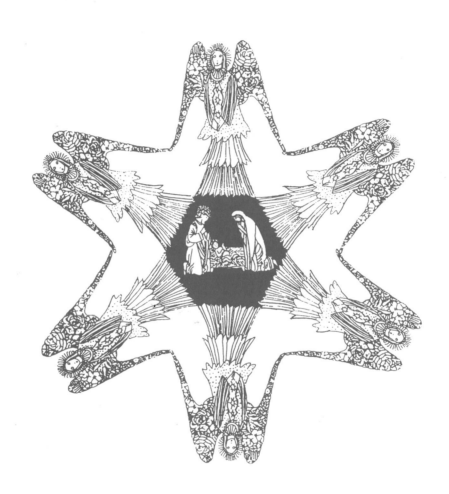